Sound Energies

By Patsy Stanley

ISBN 978-1-7322002-5-8

ISBN 7322002-5-4

LCCN 2018908830

"There is another point of view involving emanation and precipitation without personification. A sound precipitates air, then fire, then water and earth-and that's how the world becomes. The whole universe is included in this first sound, this vibration, which then commits all things to fragmentation in the field of time."

-Joseph Campbell

In Metaphysics, we pull the reality apart to get at the truth. This is basic information for studying sound energies as they apply to Metaphysical Studies.

"Because everything is made of sound, everything carries the universal urge to create more sound. Sound energies call in the angels to calibrate the energies. Different sounds call in different angels…"

-Patsy Stanley

What is Sound?

Sound is a specific type of energy created by vibrations. Objects vibrate in the air particles. When these objects vibrate, it causes the particles to "bump into other particles close to them. This movement is called sound waves. In dry <u>air</u> at 0 °C (32 °F), the speed of sound is 331.2 meters per second (1,087 ft/s; 1,192 km/h; 741 mph; 644 km). At 20 °C (68 °F), the speed of sound is 343 meters per second (1,125 ft/s; 1,235 km/h; 767 mph; 667 km), or a kilometer in 2.91 s or a mile in 4.69 s.

Scientists are now beginning to understand more about the properties of the sound energies emerging from the polarized combinations of Light/ Dark--Motion/Matter--Male/Female, and Proton/Electron that have been emerging from the "Big Bang", the first explosion of sound, since the Beginning.

Sound is the Driver of every individual part of life, causing it to move towards its destiny of oneness and understanding with the Universe. Everything has a part of itself that is constantly in touch with, and responding to the sounds of the Universe.

The Study of Sound Energies

Everything is made of sound. Therefore, we are made of sound. Each sound of the Sanskrit alphabet has a corresponding vibration in our body and each letter of the Sanskrit alphabet corresponds to at least fifty different parts of the body. Sanskrit is one of the root, or beginning languages our current languages evolved from. Sanskrit is considered to be one of the refined, or "High" languages used in India for religious studies.

Qabalah is an ancient mystical Hebrew science that studies the Letters, the Word and the Language in order to bring in more spiritual realizations. The Qabalah is connected to the organizing

1

of the sound energies that make up the hierarchies of the angelic orders. These higher, or holy, sounds are used by all religions throughout the world to maintain their belief systems. All systems contain both negative and positive energy charges, or magnetic and electric energy charges.

The Qabulah, (sometimes spelled other ways), is a group of sounds that affect the upper realms each individual part of life-us too-is attached to. Each particular group of sound energies affects the Etheric web, in order to activate and encourage attachment to each beings ancient coding-DNA; to attempt to reach personal enlightenment.

The study of sound energies is called the study of Tantra in certain areas of India, and in the Tibetan religious orders. It is said that Hue-mans have at least seven chakras. (The amount changes depending on which belief system you are looking at.) The chakras and their spinning; each petal on each chakra is considered to be composed of crystallized sound energies, whirling and putting its sound out into the world, out into the universe.

The Universal principles of life, how life moves, what life consists of, all work through sound energies. If consciousness is behind an activity, there will be sound. Whose consciousness? If not yours, them something or someone else's.

The **assimilation process** starts when we are held to our parent's,(or whoever fulfills that role for us,)chest or bosom after being born. We feel their body rhythms, and listen to the rhythm of their chemistry and heart sounds/inner world, and the outer words/outer worlds of form. The sound vibrations from the inner and the outer pour into us, forming layers that provide the formation of the abilities we will use all our lives to keep creating the universe we all carry both within and outside of ourselves. That's all done through sound. Very powerful!

2

It is when we are held in that place that we first create our own personal spaces–places we build for future times. For example, a baby or child may build a space they won't occupy until they are, thirty, forty, fifty years old.

The structuring of space to use in old age is included too, though it is usually weaker because at the child's young age in this lifetime, the experience of old age is too far away for a child to comprehend unless someone wise directs the child to, through imagination, build a mansion for its old age, without the emotional content being examined. A child imagines old age as a a return to a childlike way of being, with all the same services and approvals. Deliberate dreaming is about creating our personal –and others- three-dimensional sacred geometry. The structuring of the sacred geometry of the child has begun.

Boundaries, higher thinking, and inspiration are informed through lullabies, or reading, whatever takes the place of those, become the mantras of childhood, creating sound energy seals. The groups of sounds that are acquired at different ages, inform the moral order of the child and begin to organize it throughout all of its ages. This structuring informs the angelic orders of what protection and sanctity is needed for that hue-man being. It is a very tidy and highly organized unseen personal energy system from beginning to end.

A Mantra for You and your Children

The chakras resonate to the vowels. Here is a fine, gentle, powerful mantra that affects all of the seven chakras starting from the top down.

- ¬ Eee as in wheat- crown
- ¬ Ih- as in interest- the brow
- ¬ Eh-as in whether- the throat
- ¬ a-as in absolute- the collarbone area
- ¬ ah- as in father- the chest
- ¬ aw-as in awful-the diaphragm-
- ¬ oh- as in smoke- the belly
- ¬ ooo-as on smooth- the root

In the beginning, was the Word, and from the Word, came the Light and the Dark.

 The sounds we have on this planet are only a tiny portion of the sounds that exist throughout the universe. The oceans, the Earth we stand on, the air we breathe, and the fires that keep us warm, the food we eat, are sounds that make up their own songs.

Each plant, each blade of grass, each rock, is a container of sound. Everything reaches out through its song to praise the universe it is a part of, and the universe reaches back to it through its songs. (A celestial maintenance program)

Every hue-man being is a body of sounds, a grouping of chemical soup made of elements and light. Different parts of hue-mans hum with sound, just like everything else in creation. We are interwoven strands of sound. A living orchestra, we hum with sound all the time; different sounds come from the different parts of us, just as it does for everything else.

Sound energies are the giving forth of the blended energies of the two halves of the life force, the Proton and the Electron in atomic structure. Our reality lies within the vast sea of the two forces combined energy outpouring. Out of their associations, our reality and countless others are formed. Our reality is but a small dot of sound on the larger map of stars, galaxies, universes, planets.

When Motion and Matter come together, the energy from their interaction is sent to the neutron, where it becomes sound and is given forth. The neutron sits in the middle of the atom, and is not considered to be an active force because it is balanced – it is electro-magnetic.
The differing amounts of Colors/father and Elements/mother carry genetically, and the relationship they are having between them dictates our own personal sound range.

Ether

Ether is the fifth element. It governs from the higher soul body on up. In the higher realms, there is no form, because the vibration is so rapid. In those realms, we are becoming One again. The Universe out there doesn't recognize or speak our languages. It recognizes ideas and intention, instead. It recognizes our drivers, what moves us. Hue-mans on planet Earth have not developed an adequate soul language yet, but are striving towards it through our evolutionary processes.

Here on Earth, we have individuals with many differences, causing problems that seem insurmountable. Religions around the world are convinced they each have the only solution to our issues, causing havoc to our evolutionary processes. We are in the early stages of learning how to develop a universal language that we can all understand and use effectively to communicate with each other. Language of the soul is three dimensional, and is always concerned with pointing out to us how we are alike, not how we are different.

Music is a part of the universal language. The feeling nature is the vehicle the soul uses to express itself and connect.

We, as human beings, use verbal communication, words, which are symbols for concepts we wish to communicate to one another in symbolic forms.

Nature has its own system of symbols for its concepts and the different languages it speaks through. For example, in Nature, crickets' sounds may symbolize our lower bodies, and the throat of everything may be symbolized by bells, and the crown of the head through horns.

Energy hierarchies calibrate and work on all of the levels of sound energy vibrations, from the Beginnings through the Endings. They refine, direct, and calibrate the exact amounts of sound energies to send each part of the life they are serving within the realities maintained by the two forces. All of this is done in an organized, dynamic fashion.

Time Warps

All Time warps are achieved through sound. Time works differently in each place on Earth. On Earth, during the 80's, time was moving 40 times as fast as it had been 20 years before that. Who knows what speed time is moving at and where to these days?

Consciously and unconsciously, human beings have always studied the two energy systems and how they work together. Humans have assigned the rulers of the energy hierarchies, the Beings who calibrate the energies of those systems many names, including Gods and Goddesses, Angels, Devas, Demons, Spirit Guides, Archangels, Mid World, The Realms of Chance, etc.

The Gods and Goddesses were the mythology containers through which the different parts of the life force were once poured through and examined. The belief in one God, or one limited group of sound energies and how they work, has resulted in a even more limited personal mythologies; it is a belief that keeps us from discovering and refining more of the different aspects of the higher nature we are a part of.

Every Spiritual Philosophy and Religion develops sounds specific to it and assigns names to the energy Hierarchies that govern them. Those names are important, because they carry the organized sound energies that resonate to that part of the energy systems that govern that belief system and its place in Life. In turn, that group of sounds is a part of the larger Life Force.

7

All mythologies are based on how the elements and light systems work together. Our concepts and beliefs about a greater spiritual power is a direct reflection of our personal mythology of how the dual nature of energy is combined and provided to us.

Architecture is organized frozen sound comprised of both awe and the structural manifestations of Hue-mans.

The Body's Harmonics

Music is the artwork of the sound family.

Acupuncture and oriental medicines are based the grid theory. Grid points intersect throughout our bodies, at least every one and a half inches. Harmonics occur at those lay lines crossings, creating spinning spheres of sound. At each of the grids intersections reside stable, non-roaming spheres of resonance, seats of three-dimensional sound, governed by Angels.

Character Development

Those spinning harmonics throw off sound, which causes motion, which in turn causes us to expand and connect into more dimensions of sound.

The letters of our specific alphabet resonate to the energies that reside at those intersections. Colors run horizontal. Elements run vertical. They cross each other, and at that crossing intersection, a specific sound based on our DNA, which carries our coded ancestry of Colors and Elements is emitted.
At the intersection of each meridian in each part of our bodies, soul, mental, astral and physical, resides a character attribute in a stage of development. Issues clump around specific areas of the bodies, because of the developmental process of each attribute or characteristic during a lifetime. Issues develop character. Blocked energy is an issue in the process of being worked out.

8

Without our issues, we could not manifest onto Earth. Issues are Matter, and we have to have Matter to manifest here. We choose our issues, our Matter, both positive and negative, then we show up and experience them, for better or worse.

They become the coat of many colors we don upon initiation onto planet Earth. (All Matter or Elements work with different color energies) We made a covenant with Earth about how our character development would go, and what patterns would be worked out for each "issue" it is going to take to further our character development.

That's the purpose of issues. Then, when everything is in place, we received our first Earth Initiation onto the planet. Birth. And the character development process began.

Languages and Cultures

At least eight complex layers of energies are constantly creating the sphere every culture resides in. Each language spoken in each area of the world is a collective representation of the people living there, and where they are at on the evolutionary scale, as defined through the soul, mental, physical and emotional lives they have lived and are living now.

Each culture's group of sounds addresses the specific parts of life that are most important to them. Those basic sounds energies are woven of the karmic Intention and the soul desires of the group. What they wish to achieve in that area as a group.

The inflections in a culture's languages mirror the intentions of that culture. The inflections emphasize the goal oriented energy of that culture. The form a language takes, dictates the concepts of that culture. Those concepts fit in with the planetary chakra sounds given off in the area the culture lives in. Combinations of sound define time. Time is utilized differently each place in the universe, and in each place on planet Earth, and by each group of beings living in that area.

9

Our Speaker Systems

Our bodies are made of sound. Our chakras are the speaker systems for those sounds. Each chakra processes different sounds.
We are genetically coded and patterned to respond differently to specific groups of sounds. Whether we accept sounds or exclude them and our reactions to them, depend on our conditioned responses to certain sounds, our cultural mythologies, and our family genetics. Music is one of the easier ways to introduce all to new energies.

Languages

The oldest recorded languages carry the essence of the history of humanity as well as its many different aspects. Languages become more magnetic as they age, and eventually reside in sound banks. All generations add to these sound banks. These stored essences become very pure and powerful over long periods of time.

It is said that the older the Word, the greater the possibility of healing or destroying the Self, or the World at large.

The study of sound energies may be the ultimate search for The Holy Grail, the First Word that the universe resonated to in its oneness.

All cultures work with different groups of sound energies. Each culture defines the Duality, the color and elemental energies residing in that area, in their specific way through sound. Each culture assigns the location of their sounds according to their group needs, so that what we perceive in one culture as valid assignment of sound energy structures and how they operate, may not be valid for another culture.

10

Everything has its own language that it expresses its experience of life through. Since the beginning, languages have been developed by humans and all other species to communicate with each other.

These languages define themselves around each group of people, or species, particular adaptations and needs. Each culture adapts the usage of things in their environment to make the sounds they need, such as music instruments.

The Mystery Schools

When a language becomes written, a history is developed to explain the sound usage in the language. Sound has been used for many purposes down through the centuries by human beings, from shouting to knock down walls or singing to a child or sweetheart.

The spiritual study of sound energies and how to use them as tools, has been going on in large and small ways since hue-mans became aware of the concept of the Self and its relationship to God.

The Mystery Schools have taught sound energies and their power and uses since their inception. Sound energies are the most powerful energies on the planet.

- ¬ Can heal with sound
- ¬ Can transfer attributes
- ¬ Can work with anything in life with sound energies

It's a matter of learning how to manipulate the sounds, work with them and direct them towards an end.

Earth Chakras and Their Sounds

The Earth is a living Entity with its own sounds pouring through its own chakras. The Earth has lay lines, a meridian grid structure, and many energy vortexes and paths. Those energies are composed of groups of sounds that carry the potential for health, character development, and many other possibilities for humans living in specific areas.

The polarities of sound reverse depending on the areas they are in, thus changing the directions and seasons. The "family" or ecosystems in each of these areas are all part of the sound systems that make up the whole. The Earth resonates at an overall vibration. Within that vibration are different vibrations. Mountains vibrate differently than oceans. Plants and animals have their own vibrations.

The Earth is experiencing itself as a living entity, just as we are, and it stores the essences of those experiences in different parts of itself, just as we do with our bodies. Earth sounds are created and stored and emit from meridian crossings, just like with humans.

The places on the Earth's grid where the color energies and the elemental energies intersect, produce specific sounds that are maintained in that area. The amount and usage and power of the sounds develop from the size and location of the intersection.
Many of the sounds in these areas are held in specific forms in Nature. Frozen architecture, Whirlpools, geysers, the North and South poles, etc., all express and maintain these. The kinds of stones, crystals, minerals, soils, plants, and the animals that live in that area, are all part of the group of sound energies overseen by the Energy Beings in that area. If any part of it becomes extinct, a part of the voice of God is lost.
When enough of the plants, animals, and other forms residing in an area become extinct, the humans living in that ecological area lose their roots and become emotional nomads.

Our Place on Earth

The lay lines in each area of this planet define and hold the energy patterns for each culture of humans living there, giving them the sounds that formulate their language, their feelings, how they think, and how they view the world.

Everyone on this planet has a place or places that correspond to the sounds of their being. Earth provides specific positive and negative areas for all the parts of life that reside on it.

Cultures are formed and located geographically around specific combinations of the Earths sounds. It is no accident that we live where we live, and that we move to other places as we change. The particular culture or cultures, each person is born into has sound energies that are specific to it-them- that are contained by the culture (s)in that area. If we move away from that area, we lose direct access to experiencing those sound energies and the Hierarchies that govern them. However, we can return to those places quickly through memories and our early sound energy trainings.

The energies where we were born or grew up always have a specific purpose and goal, but they may or may not have harmonized with our own personal sound energies, and our own personal purposes and goals. If they don't, then we might need to move to a different place, where the sound energies may better match our needs, creating greater freedom and improved health.

Sound Energy Banks

Each culture's language contains the essence of its past experiences as a whole culture. This essence is contained in the vowel structure of the language. The silence between words contains the history of the emotional content of the culture. As new experiences occur, the essences of those new experiences are added to the culture's sound energy storage banks, causing the language of that culture to be experienced on the older energy lanes we each carry, such as the soul planes. As the sound bank of the culture slowly evolves, we resonate or respond to it on a deeper level.

Changing a Language

Sound vibrations come before the structural aspects of language. Structure is linear, it focuses on time and space and organizes it into meaningful activities with a purpose and goal. Consonants structure the language, while the emotional content lies in the vowel usage and the silences between words in the language. The history of emotional content lies in the silence between words. Those silences are extremely magnetic and packed full of meanings. If we look at where the structure came from, it history, its resonances mean more to us and we can attach and understand better.

Whenever an oral language is brought into written form, a large part of the essence of the past emotional experiences and their purpose and meanings defined as to that culture, is lost. That is because it is being re-structured.

The new group of experiences will be formed into a written language, forcing the emotional content and its history to develop a more linear, masculine polarity.

The feminine aspect of a language is the essence of the experiences contained within the words, the vowels. The feminine aspect is always circular, and many times, has no language available to explain itself because of the depth of the essences it contains. This depth is caused by age, and speaks the languages of the soul and the ancients.

In circular cultures, indigenous, Native American, etc.,(death) endings, and (life) beginnings, are always connected. You can't have one without the other. It takes two cheeks to make a butt. Beginnings and endings take place at the same time. What ends begins again. That is the circle of life. Circularity is non-goal oriented because of this, and is as everything else is, dual natured.

Father energies

Patriarchal religions work with linear energies. They work with consonants – structure and rules are most important.

The method and style we use to express the Air and Fire Elements, the projective forces, the patterning for this is passed on to us by our father.

Our relationship with our father and the way he used his sound energies, controls and directs the way we use them. Fathers teach their children how to express within each body, not how to connect the bodies one to another, so that relationship occurs. Mother does that. Father's teach the principles of Individuation. The masculine proton force of projection provided by father, actively clears energies. It is stimulating, forceful, and active, and can pinpoint things. This energy has authority over all of our forms of communication, verbalization and all forms of self-expression.

Sounds leave and go out. They find the energy that matches, and brings it back to us. This is the force at work in life that allows change to happen.

15

The expression of the choices you make about how life is going to take place for you, lies in this process. Father's patterning overlays the liver and its systems in our physical bodies.

Mother

Matriarchal energies work with vowels and the silence between letters of the alphabet – the content and its meaning.

The method and style we use to experience the Water and Earth Elements, the patterns we have for receiving sounds, and our boundaries around that, are given to us by our Mother.

The way we related to our mother, and the way she used her energies, that pattern governs how we use those energies. The same pattern rules the way our bodies are connected one to another, how they relate, and how we experience them.

Mother patterned us for how to experience life, how to connect to anything, and how connection works. She taught us how to receive. She gave us the patterning for receiving and what sounds to accept, which senses to use first and when, and how long we should use them.

Our patterning for the receiving and experiencing of sound is given to us through our Mother, and the way she experienced Life. The experiences we let into our lives are governed by Mother's patterns. These patterns allow the sounds into the system that will assist that specific part of life to maintain itself and exclude all other sounds.

Through this principle, introduction of new sounds into the system are regulated in order for growth to be maintained. Mother's patterns overlay the kidney and spleen systems in our physical bodies.

16

The parts of each body works with different letters. The different bodies work with a different music octave, for example. We respond to different sounds in each body, those being the soul, mental, astral, and physical bodies we are speaking of for our purposes.

Sounds move at different speeds. Each letter of each alphabet vibrates at different speeds. The rate of vibration causes our names to be located on different energy planes and in different bodies, and to reside in different time frames. This is how memories are made and stored.

The physical body is the interwoven patterns of sound attached to the organic matter of our first name. They are the lowest and slowest sounds in vibration or motion in our four bodies. This energy resides in "now" time.

Our middle name is the interwoven patterns of sound attached to the matter of our astral body. No middle name? No pattern to cling to emotionally, means there is no named (specific sound energies) form to "gel" to on that energy level. They have chosen to have a great deal of freedom in the astral/emotional realms along with a great deal of fear and insecurity at times. It is the Word chosen for the emotional experiencing during this **lifetime**.

The Mental Body

Our last name, our father's name, is made up of the interwoven patterns of sound of the higher part of our mental body that resides just below the lower soul planes of energy. It is our personal chosen Word for the **future time** we reside in this lifetime.

The Soul Body

Our mother's maiden name contains the spiritual history of the bodies we now have. That name carries the developed energies of the causal body. **It is the personal Word for the unconscious part of the self in any given lifetime.**

In any name, the capital letters are the most predominant and powerful. They carry a lot more energy in them. People set up their names for the capital letters, because capitals carry the basic essence of the ribbons of light that particular body is made out of.

If we lay out our names with the letters and their meanings, they can give us information on what our intentions and patterns might be. We can also use these letters to know more about the energies of anything that has ever been named.

All letters carry different energies, both positive and negative. All the letters can be negative as well as positive. Some are more powerful when they are negative.

Be careful about working with these energies because of the power of them. When we use sound energies, we are quadrupling the energies we are putting out!

To make words more positive, bring them into the front of the face, don't hold them in the back of the throat. The sounds will be smoother and higher.

The following letters, depending on the elements each one is attached to, can heal as many as three parts of the body at the same time. For example, if the letter works with the elements of air, water, and ether, it will work in three different areas of the body and its organs.

All our bodies each have different healing needs. They are interwoven, so the healing desired can be needed by any one of them, physical, astral, mental, or soul.

Do not work with these sounds on your own unless you understand the concept of each letter and what it will do to you. They are too powerful to use without training.

When working with sound energies for healing organs, pull it directly into the part you are trying to heal. The body responds quickest to slow, gentle energy. It is a gentle system. Use small doses.

The following is a basic sound energy chart, listing letters of the American English alphabet and their meanings. All languages, down through time, go through changes that affect their power and meaning.

¬ **A**..ahhh sound
- ♣ color: light blue
- ♣ element: air
- ♣ anus and lungs
- ♣ Musical note: G

If you pull in this concentrated sound energy for the lungs, you will feel a heat expansion, and it will heal that part of the body. You will hear it mentally as you work with it. It can be expressed verbally with the outward breath. It is hard to breathe the "ahhh" sound in, so just hear it mentally. 'A' energy that works with awareness, awakening, clairaudience, levitation, reasoning, perception, cognition of profound truths. Atlantis era set this sound energy.

With this letter, you will be drawing in the energies that allow absorption of all of the attributes, and the use of them at will. This is transmuting lead into gold, and bringing the dead back to living. This is working with magic, alchemy, musical gifts, eloquence, and poetic talent. This letter works with understanding the language of symbols and their command and power.

¬ **B ..buzzing sound, softly vibrate lips**
- o color: light violet
- o element: water
- o right eye
- o Musical note: A

This letter works with balance, duality, and the electro-magnetic fluids. B works with understanding of the concept of negative as well as positive, and cognition of polarity in all forms of existence. This letter works with learning that the entire realm of duality is always blending. B works with intuition

- ¬ **C..sounds like a hiss, and made while smiling**
  - o color: vermillion red-
  - o element: fire
  - o stomach
  - o Musical note: D

This letter works with the Mystery of The Eucharist, the Body and the Blood of Christ, and transference of ability to another person, or to transfer abilities to another person. During the act of eating, one is in a state of At-One-Ment with the world.

- ¬ **D..*zzz* sound made behind front teeth**
  - o color: dark blue
  - o element: earth
  - o right ear
  - o Musical note: C

This letter works with discernment, bringing things into form. Form planning for later manifestation, organizes, eliminates procrastination, gives drive and determination. This letter works with all the Mysteries of Creation, inner and outer. D works with the magic of love, all methods of Magic, sex Magic, and makes the aspects of all the four elements available for access and practice. D works with learning to master love in all its aspects. **DA.. works with the will to live, and is a life force energy.**

- ¬ **E.. eeeeee**
  - o Color: dark violet
  - o element: fire
  - o spinal column
  - o Musical note: D

E works with transference of consciousness, sobering up, intoxication, union with universal consciousness and highest forms of intuition on the soul levels, and with enthusiasm. E-works with materialization and de-materialization. Can also work with other people who have been drinking.

- ¬ **F.. fouf.. bring upper front teeth and bottom lip together. Puff up cheeks and breathe F through your teeth and lower lip.**
  - o Color: light green
  - o element: water
  - o left hand
  - o Musical note is F#

Focuses energy to a single point. Collects scattered energy. F works with polarity, harmonizing, balancing, legalities, and will energy. F works with blending the consciousness of the lower bodies with the higher bodies. When F people go negative, they have no focus and become very scattered. Fear and frustration.

- ¬ **G.. sound made in back of throat**
  - o color: green
  - o element: earth
  - o left eye
  - o Musical note: F

G works with abundance, grace and manifestation, divine grace, feelings of happiness and complete satisfaction, all phases of wealth, riches, and happiness.

- **H..cat hissing sound**
  - color: silvery violet
  - element: water
  - right arm
  - Musical note: A

H works with the power of the Word and inner sight that sees things as they really are. It helps us cut through the illusions. Use H for clarity when confused. Can use H energy to look at a situation and see it as it really is, not as it appears to be. H helps us with understanding of universal language, purest clairvoyance, and is a fine tuning to improve ability to hear.

- **I..long iiii sound, no ee**
  - Color: light opal, which is a myriad of colors that have an opalescent feeling to them.
  - element: earth
  - left kidney
  - Musical note: G

I works with self-identity and the ability to image. I works with tracking energy on the inner levels, with tracking it back to its source. Memory and consciousness, including past life, Photographic memory. Works with everything that has shape and dimension and that can be counted.

- **J.. say it as is**
  - color: dark opal
  - element: earth
  - diaphragm and solar plexus
  - Musical note: G#

J works with love and joy. Ability of Mastery to evoke or diminish love or sympathy at will, and increasing sexual energy.

- **K..kksssss**
  - color: silvery blue
  - elements: air and fire
  - left ear
  - Musical note: B

This is the first of the Mastery letters. It works with letters A-K. It is a very powerful sound energy to have in a name. When it is negative, it is extremely negative. When it is positive, it is extremely positive. K- works with the liver and spleen, adrenals and kidneys.

K works with faith, knowing, courage, and endurance. Working with this energy can help miracles to happen on inner or outer.

- **L..like the way love sounds.**
  - Color: dark green
  - element: air
  - chest
  - Musical note: F

L works with youth, rejuvenation, health, beauty, harmony, and is the fountain of youth. Those who work with the L sound come to realize that we don't have light unless we have shadows. This is a kind of understanding of the duality of life.

- **M..mmmmmmmm**
  - color: blue green
  - element: water
  - abdomen
  - Musical note: D

M works with the mothering energy, manifestation, nurturing, Mastery of magnetic fluids, and it works with the magnetic principles.

¬ N..nnnnnnn
- o color: flesh colored brick red
- o element: fire
- o liver
- o Musical note: A

N works with happiness, negativisms, loneliness, isolation, fear, and anger.

¬ O.. ooooh
- o color: blue fire
- o element: fire
- o Musical note: C

pharynx and throat-O works with order, legality, everything falls into place, I see, and the functioning of the electro-magnetic fluids in the body.

¬ P..pppp airy sound
- o color: dark gray
- o element: earth
- o right side of nose
- o Musical note is B

P works with power, purification, purity, purifies cells in the body, brings peace, being in touch with divine love, and profound humility. If you are toxic, work with P energy to purify cells in the body.

¬ Q.. quuuuu
- o color: magenta
- o element: water, fire, and ether
- o Q does not work with a specific part of the body.

Q works with questioning, inquisitiveness, and questing. Q energy is linked up with U energy and has a lot of attributes of U. Sound is KU. Q works with K energy.

Q and V are not considered to have their own specific attributes.

- ¬ **R..rrrrrrrrrr**
  - o color: molten gold, looks like thick, melted liquid gold.
  - o Element: water
  - o left side of nose
  - o Musical note: C

R works with freedom and independence, the ability to warp time, and the ability to work with distortions of time and space. R energy speeds up time.

When you work with someone resistant and rigid, work with R energy to get it and turn it around; will be an 'R' revolutionary person that supports freedom and expansion-could turn into an amazing person.

- ¬ **S..ssss with closed lips.**
  - o Color: purple red
  - o element: fire
  - o gallbladder
  - o Musical note: G#

S energy works with developing third eye sight, strong power, will energy, and the electric fluids in the body. One can pull this energy in through fire finger, and direct it to dissipate illusion. Works with the gift of prophecy; works with highest divine virtue.

¬ **T..tssss**
- o Color: brownish black
- o Element: earth
- o right kidney
- o Musical note: F

T works with mastering control of elements, time tracking. Someone with lots of T's in their name can learn how to go back and forth in time really easily. To use this time track: go on other levels and will see plane of light with different tracks on it. Usually go to center track and can go forward or backward in time –can just drop down – tracks in center are usually more accurate- Example- go 5 years ahead in time, drop down and see what's happening in yours or someone else's life, hard to read our own. Works with mechanical memory — like a rolodex — mind can work this way.

¬ **U..uuuuuuuuu**
- o Color: shiny black
- o Element: earth and ether
- o pancreas
- o Musical note: B

U works with union and connection with God, union in all aspects, and understanding, and astral projection.

¬ **V.. vvvv without ee, softly**
- o Color: silvery green
- o Element: earth, water
- o no specific body part
- o No specific musical note

V is the second of the mastery letters. V works with K-V. V works with understanding beyond the realm of your control in your life. It is very expansive. V works with W energy.
Q and V are not considered to have their own specific attributes.

27

- ¬ **W... say it as it is**
  - o Color: lilac
  - o element: air
  - o whole abdomen from duodenum to rectum, no specific area
  - o Musical note: G

Very good for manifesting, concentrating an ability, wisdom and wonder. W is good technique to use for manifesting. Decide the space and time for when you want to manifest. See what you want as happening. Use a lot of m's and w's, weird, wild, wonderful, magic, mysterious, then release it at once, if you don't, it won't work.

- ¬ **X..make a k sound in throat**
  - o color: peachy with dark red
  - o elements: fire, earth, ether
  - o no specific area
  - o No specific musical note

X works with WORDS - exorcism, expectations, expelling, existence, exuberance, and exhilaration.

- ¬ **Y.. say as is, y**
  - o Color: pink
  - o Element: fire
  - o heart
  - o Musical note: C#

Y works with prophecy, union with God, cosmic love, intuition, and inspiration.

¬ **Z.. say as is zzz (bumblebee sound)**
- o   color: lemon yellow
- o   element: air
- o   heart
- o   Musical note: G

Z works with humor, past life memory, and money power. A perverse sense of humor.

The application of sound energies creates alternative destinies.

The following is a few of the many possible Letter combinations:
- **K-V-X** all deal with the endocrine system.
  - pineal,
  - pituitary,
  - thyroid,
    thymus

OE-
- written this way – Ö
- pronounced owoehee
- orange; fire
- ability to change energy from one energy to another-transmutation
- affects
  - ♣ testicles
  - ♣ ovaries
  - ♣ works to clear out blocks

- **AJ-**
  - mental enthusiasm,
  - dark opal/light blue

- **Th-** pronounce this-
  - indigo-ether-
  - will,
  - thought,
  - motivating power

- **Ea-**
  - eeeahah blended-
  - reddish orange- fire & ether-
  - calming, releasing of tension

- **St- sta,**
  - stop-Blazing red, fire
  - original power
  - ecstasy
  - shields
  - Negative is stuck, stubborn

- **Ae- aaaeee-**
  - light brown-earth-
  - mastery of negative beings
- makes things grow

  -

  - sparkling deep violet purple- ether-
  - ability with language & communication
  - building channels
  - power,
  - mastery

- **Be-** Buu bull-
  - brownish black-
  - block energy
  - blending
  - bleach energies white
  - destroy negative being with rod of power

- **cl- clll-**
  - dark green- silver
  - air; water; ether
  - clearing
  - cleansing
  - clarity
  - if confronted with illusion, use cl to get clarity

31

- ¬ **wh- wha-**
    - o white ether
    - o cleans out dark energy
    - o whitens energy
    - o use in combination with black

- ¬ **sh –**
    - o blue/violet purple-
    - o ether-air-
    - o shields

Each letter works with a specific organ as well as a part of the body.

The five vowels we have in our language are connected to our five senses:

See- E
Hear-O
Touch-A
Smell-U
taste – I

To see on the energy planes is an electric activity.

The note E- improves sight

Assimilation of information is magnetic; it involves each of our senses in different ways.

Vowels are connected to our senses, and express our inner experiences.

Vowels contain the essence of each cultures experiences. Consonants express those experiences.

Each culture assigns the properties of vowels in their language according to the essence of the past experiences contained within them, therefore, connection works differently in all groups.

Vowels are the feminine aspect of any language. The shamanic energy system is ancient and contains many useful healing sound energy paths that are stored in humanities' old memories. These sounds are the symbols of the unconscious organizing itself.
Consonants work with the outer meridian structures.
Consonants are outer experiences

Consonants boundarize time and set time frames. Structures endings and beginnings. Consonants set the structure, using time as its frame of reference, to contain the vowels.

Consonants keep time contained in a particular reality.

The essence of the experience contained in vowels, are maintained in a particular reality by the surrounding use of consonants.

The Bible

The Naming process is both planetary and universal for all things. It is through the naming process that Manifestation takes place. When energy is directed to a conceived end, it must go there.

In Genesis, the Naming may be about assigning specific sound energies to beginnings.

In Genesis, Adam and Eve "named" everything in the Garden. In doing so, they set in place the basic sound energies for that particular reality. In Genesis, God gave them permission to do the naming.

If you are of a different religious persuasion or have a different way of viewing spirituality, you have your own religious "naming" stories and concepts.

We have an inborn, natural desire to name the parts of life around us. This desire is both inherited and natural, both spiritual and mundane. We all have individual patterns for the naming process through the sounds that have been encoded in our family systems and our generations. By nature, each family system includes certain groups of sounds and excludes others.

Different sounds emit from different parts of us, just as it does from the objects and people around us. A rock or other object that we are attracted to and carry around, has a hum – a sound. That's why we chose it. The meaning it has for us comes through our perceived connection to its experience.

All sounds contained in belief systems eventually become rigid and have to change. This is where religions struggle to adapt. All language changes throughout time in order to adapt to the new experiences and expressions going on in the universe and on this planet. All generations keep adding to the sound bank.

The Power of Silence

The space between each spoken word contains its own silent language. The space, or silence, between each letter of the every alphabet spoken, is the glue that holds the Word together.

Pentecostal "speaking in tongues" in the evangelical religions and other ecstatic languages, may represent the speaking out of past life languages that weren't expressed during that life time…an expression coming from the unconscious higher self.

The few societies we've had access to and studied, who think in a nonlinear fashion, appear to exist in realities we cannot understand. Ancient mythical must be meditated up on to be understood. If the universe is a circle, everything inside is also outside. The Universe cannot be unraveled like a ball of yarn.

Consciousness focuses differently when you put yourself in it without making it accommodate you.

Sound can be used consciously to create chaos or order in the world.

Two Monasteries in Tibet went to war with each other. They used sound energies as their weapons against each other. Within a short time, both monasteries lay in ruins.

Sometimes, something startles us so that we expand and remember that everything outside us is a reflection of the universe inside us.

There is an old story of a child being invited to look down an Elder's throat. The child saw stars and galaxies and a universe when he looked inside. He saw rivers and brooks and grass and trees. He saw the Elder's family as they had been for a thousand years, and all of the things they had together and apart. He saw all the good and bad things they had done with each other. He saw a sun and he saw darkness, but he could not hear. He was spared hearing the sounds so that he could live…

J.R.R. Tolkein

"There was Eru, the One, who in Arda is called Illu'vatar:
And he made first the Ainur, the Holy Ones, that were the off spring of his thought, and they were with him before aught else was made.
And he spoke to them, propounding to them themes of music: and they sang before him and he was glad. But for a long time, they sang only each alone, or but few together, while the rest hearkened: for each comprehended only that part of the mind of Illu'vatar from which he came, and in the understanding of their brethren, they grew but slowly. Yet ever as they listened they came to deeper understanding, and increased in unison and harmony..."

Examples of the harmonic process.

Mantras

A mantra repeats sounds given forth in a repeated circular cycle. People as well as buildings, animals, minerals, and groups of plants have mantras. Those sounds maintain those Forms. Each chakra in everything has a spiritual path it follows. The more you are immersed in a deliberate mantra, the more vowels it will contain. The more vowels, the more emotional content, adding more meaning on all of the energy levels. The more the meaning, the deeper the energy path becomes, and the more it is rooted and manifesting.

- ¬ Dark blue- works with D
- ¬ Green earth works with G
- ¬ Light Opal- works with I
- ¬ Dark Opal works with J-gigi
- ¬ Dark Gray works with P

Music

We use "Name That Tune!" to get spontaneity...The songs of a culture and of its individuals, mirror their ability to connect and separate. When sound is put into song form, its impact is more connective than when it is spoken. Music reflects, and comes before external influences take place.

Music is the sound of the mind working. Through song, we feel understood and a part of it all.

The Catholic church documented the history of sound development through music in western society. It is the only written history of western music we have available.

From the beginning of the last century, 1900 A.D. until1973 A.D., in 73 years, the amount of music we created equaled the amount we created from 1300 A.D. to 1900 A. D. -600 years!

All music until 1300 A.D. was based on the C note. Chants only, because not enough other notes available. Monotones were focused on.

- ¬ 1400 A.D. into 1600's—Renaissance-Focused on form and texture of tones rather than containment or tonality

- ¬ 1600'—1750's: Baroque-
  - o development of three-dimensional form through sound.
- ¬ Extra used to stress past two-dimensional development into three. Container development. Rococo –

  Death of Bach-
  - o He brought mathematics into music—
  - o geometry began to correspond to sound

- 1750-1825-
  - French Classical-
  - development of classical music.
  - Connection of sound to sound without interruption or silence. Romantic period of music begins.
  - Hayden and Mozart were mathematicians and billiard players who studied geometry and added it to their music.
- 1875-
  - Wagner-Idealist—
  - Development of themes—ideas, stories, mythologies as containers for music energies.
  - Usually Nordic, with basic belief system of the myth being the salvation of man through love of a woman.
  - Schinkler analyzed symphonies down to one note.

- Until early 1900's—
  - rigid development through mathematics of "harmony" through shape and form.
  - Music was emotionally correct.
- 1900's forward—
- Tones became much more harmonic and lush. They resonated with our chakra systems.

Around 1973, with the development of synthesized or "canned" music, we went into fast time and lost the connection to natural sound. Synthetic sound produces pitches not contained in tonal scales. The focus is on form and texture, not on tonality or feeling.

Music has not been able to be contained nor measured since the development of the synthesizer, a machine that has replaced the human connection through sound to the feeling nature
From that time forward, we have not had time to use our internal formulating processes, we have had to do it externally.

SHAKE NOTES: Toning for Sacred Purposes

Shake notes and their tones are the closest application western culture used for sacred purposes:

In the 1800's, pianos in churches were rare. You have to have "pitch", or a frame of reference, to be able to hit any note, so "shake" notes were put in hymnals.

Our bodies respond to all sounds. It is the nature of us to do so as a part of life. It is also natural for each individual person to hit different notes, so there was a natural note in place in the system for each person that was easiest and most powerful for them to tone from.

The notes were squares, triangles, circles, and hollows. Each one of these symbols denoted: Do, re, mi, fa, so, la ,ti do. The people singing, then knew what note to sound through this visualization technique. In the "Shaker" system, sound is focused in the facial area, instead of the throat or chest.

Each visual note was toned by the group. Visually, they took in each symbol with sacred intention, and gave it sound, giving that form energy, making it into a sacred geometric symbol. Each symbol vibrated upward into different parts of the chakra system, activating and purifying the chakras with positive sacred energy.
Using sound energies in this method ties the traditional, collective memories of the group to current time. The bringing forth into present life of each person's oldest habits and deepest memories, enabled reframing and change to take place. The Shaker people were probably not consciously aware of that effect. It was their souls that were helping them out.

Music can be divided into five basic levels of Reaction

Raw sound- pure tones:
1. Hearing with no judgement, no exclusion – It is just sound, made up of raw, pure tones.

2. 2.The imagination activates. If we listen to sound with closed eyes, the sound drops into our memory banks and evokes pictures.

3. Realities are compared through memory sorting, and putting them in their place — receiving the sound — and consciousness is altered. We receive different realities from different senses

4. The Elements evoke a connection to feeling. Sound therapies are based on this principle.

5. What are our bodies made of? Silence following the sound involves us in listening to the body's sound. To trust silence is very hard. Silence is very powerful.

In the antiquity of our own personal being lie languages and songs as old as those that have been discovered and recorded here on planet earth.

Just as each place we go has a past, underlying our being is a base of sound that supports our essence.

This essence is made up of the music our many past lives have played. That essence pours into the time we are living in today, and it is the eternal essential fertilizer for going forward.

The Musician's Palace

Music works with the green energies of the heart chakra. Each chakra has a spiritual path it follows. Musicians work at the task of blending the higher and lower natures. They serve mankind as a path to travel, a bridge between the higher and lower nature.

Corresponding Emotions in Music Notes:

We have to have a pitch, or frame of reference, before we can hit any note. That's where emotion and context come into play. Each note evokes a different set of emotions in us.

- C Major- innocence- simplicity
- C Minor- declarations of love and unrequited love. Pining away.
- Db Major-sarcasm, that falls down into grief and rapture
- D Major-shouts of triumphs, victories, rejoicing
- D Minor- melancholy womanliness, the spleen and humors brooding
- D# Minor- soul level anxieties and deepest fears. Ghosts, all fears
- Eb Major-lovely positive devotion, personal conversations with God
- E Major- noisy joyful shouts of laughter never completed, delight
- F Major- calmness, compliance
- F Minor- depression, funereal laments, groans of misery, longing for the grave
- F# Major- triumph over difficulties, sighs of heartfelt relief, echo of the soul who has fiercely struggled and finally conquered, lies in all uses of this key.
- F# Minor- a gloomy key, tugs at passion like a dog tugging at a sheet on the clothesline, resentment and discontent are its language

41

- ¬ G Major- everything rustic, idyllic and lyrical, calm, satisfied passion, tender gratitude for true love and faithful affection, every gentle and peaceful emotion of the heart is correctly expressed through this key
- ¬ G Minor- discontent, uneasy, worry about failed schemes, gnashing of teeth, resentment and dislike
- ¬ Ab Major- key of the grave, death, grave, putrefaction, judgment and eternity lie in its radius
- ¬ Ab Minor- grumbler, heart squeezed until it suffocates, wailing lament, difficult struggler, struggling with difficulties
- ¬ A Major- Declarations of love and innocent love, satisfaction with one's state of affairs, hope of seeing one's beloved again when parting, cheerfulness and trust in God
- ¬ A Minor- pious womanliness, tenderness of character
- ¬ Bb Major- cheerful love, clear conscience, aspirations for a better world.
- ¬ Bb Minor- quaint person who is somewhat surly and rarely looks pleasant, mocking God and the world, discontented with itself and everything, preparation for suicide sounds in this key.
- ¬ B Major- strong emotions, wild passions, glaring presentations, anger, rage, jealousy, fury , despair, every burden of the heart lies in this sphere.
- ¬ B Minor- patience, calm, awaiting one's fate, submission to the divine.

From The Psychology of Music.

Deliberately playing a certain note on a pitch pipe will move the energy in a specific direction.
A mother who sings to her child is relaying emotional patterns to the child. Patterning the child to react to and accept or reject the emotional music tones in life it will encounter.

The Spiral

The line and the circle form the sacred spiral of life, which is eternally in motion. Natural music instruments that resonate, that work with the Spiral of life energies are bowls, drums, and shakers. Any natural tuneful resonators draw the collective energies in the area up into a higher and larger way of thinking, because resonance affects all the parts of us, and has lingering effects. Synthetic music cannot do this.

Whole businesses are expert in creating varieties of sounds for every use, from fun to psychology and philosophy to healing:

The Basic Elements of Music

Drone- This is the bedrock upon which all other music elements rest. A long, uninterrupted sound of a natural (not canned or synthetic) single pitch can affect — touch a person in a specific area — resonance of the organ duplicated with a pitch frequency has the potential to release blockages and tension from the area.

The harmonics that naturally occur above any Drone will balance the aura and etheric — surrounding the body — while the Drone tone touches the physical center of the problem-illness. Toning is an effective use of drone sound.

Repetition-chanting-or instrument repetitiveness: creates a healing background, a receptive altered state for the healing modality, the healing work, to take place in.

Rhythm- duplicates a healthy pulse- in nature or in people; easiest to duplicate in people is the heart rate, the breathing rate, and the brain waves. Duplicate healthy rhythms, and theirs will automatically begin to follow that pulse.

Harmonics- the emotional content of music; use of music intervals can harmonize the emotions, also bring diseased organ's molecular structure into a healing process. Use to balance physical body with the other bodies.

Melody- helps transcend pain: we forget our physical body and engage the melody with our mind. Melodies evoke shapes and images; knowing the effects of the different scales is invaluable to a person using imagery and visualization to mentally reprogram the course of their illness.

Instrumental colors- all natural instruments, depending on their qualities (size, shape, purpose, etc.) vibrate in the human spirit, the human, the body and the mind.

Form- The Form or design of the music: composition decides the direction the listener travels in; can create moods, tempos, can act as a sedative (lullaby) music therapy for illnesses.

Intention- positive intentions can produce purity, give heart, be true and lasting.

There are many elements to music, for our emotions love to connect and dance.

The blues scale in music evokes despair and connection with the depths of the earth. It is a wail Form, and Wails are extremely useful for healing sorrows and for recognition of endurance. In Ireland, professional Wailers are often hired for Wakes.

To take people deeper into themselves, use Native American scales, because they're loaded with vowels.

Water element- tinkling sounds- helps things to move from one place to another.

Most music is based on the pulses that we experience through nature or our bodies. Duplicating those pulses greatly affects us.

Playing music that pulses at the beat that brain waves pulse at when in meditation, slows agitation down. Slows pulse-Duplicate with music heartbeat or breathing cycles to regulate them.

Playing music pulsed with Alpha and Theta brain waves is good for Alzheimer's patients.

There is power in music and sound.

Rhythm - Music and sound are needed in rituals to empower them. Rhythms are based on the pulses of nature and our bodies.

The beat of classical music of the Baroque Period is good for soft background music for mental body work. Or in the library!

Heavy metal or rap music — going thru puberty. This is an unconscious method used to separate from what is inevitable, learning to individuate while still knowing you are a part of it all.

Entrainment is a phenomenon that occurs when individuals or groups feel and move in the same rhythm. When they lock in and become as one being — is present everywhere in nature — when schools of fish or flocks of birds, for example, move as if they are one, this is a type of "entrainment". Energetically, it is following a fad on the astral planes.

Those songs you heard in your head? You know, the ones that "randomly" pass through? They regulate rhythm and send messages to you. Notice how all of them have words or a specific rhythm to them, until you get out in nature. Then they turn classical, and start flowing instead of start and stop.

All of Life is Singing

Music reflects and comes before external influences manifest. Music is the sound of the bodies working together. Our bodies are like an orchestra. Each of them play different instruments. Each of them have their own sheet music. Each of them need to be heard in order for the harmonics to take place.

As each of them practices their music, they become more and more aware of the other members of the orchestra they are a part of and how they can be beautiful together. Finally, they join together to learn, and then they all become aware that there is an orchestra leader. It takes awhile for the orchestra leader to get their attention and to get them to play together under leadership.

There are larger groups of sound energies surrounding us:

- the sounds of karma and dharma
- the sounds of evolution
- the sounds of involution
- Evolution goes up-- has sounds for it
- Involution goes down-has sounds for it
- Spiral created by both- have sounds to it
- The Holy Spiral is created by up and down, forming the Holy Spin, the Holy Trinity.

I heard this story once:

> That when the Word came to be, it scattered everywhere and even farther, and made a living sea of sound mixed with silence and mystery.
> I heard the story of how every living thing was given the time to strike their own note in all that is.
> And I heard it said that each star, each planet, the moon and the Earth, and you and I,

46

are living bodies evoking the power of sound and
silence, and how together, we sing the songs
of all that is because after all,
we are the choirs of Spirit,
and while we are here,
before we change form again and begin to sing
another song, we sing and love as greatly and
hugely as we can, sounds given out in trust, hope,
fear and joy, of the known and unknowable, each a
part of life, we remain forever, a child of the
Universe...

We live in a world made of sound, and finding the resonances
that works best for our energy systems is a healing thing to do
for ourselves.

There is a cosmic hum that dwells in the sound encoding of
every individual part of life. Everything hums with sound all the
time. We are amazing, beautiful interwoven strands of sounds
that are made up of all the experience and expressions we have
accumulated in our eternal life so far...

Finding your voice has many different levels. The soul does not
speak the same language as the mind, the emotions, or the
physical body. Each one is connected to each other, yet each one
has separate voices that address the different needs of the Self.

Hue-mans do not live by bread alone. All the bodies need
different sustenance. The major and minor grids of sound we are
all made of, assign spiritual, emotional, mental and physical
faculties to each part of us in each of the bodies. This assigning
of sound energies is in every culture and in every spiritual
practice throughout the world.

Be the Singer

This is an excellent exercise, short and sweet, and done to quickly recapture your joy and your balance. And in the doing, we will learn about laughter and retune our Toning properties:

1. Pick a song you liked to sing when you were a child.
2. Sing the song again, louder in some places, whispering in others.
3. Stop singing at different places in the song for a few seconds.
4. Sing the song using a fake foreign accent.
5. Sing it again, using invented words instead of the song's words.
6. Pretend you are singing the song to your sweetheart.
7. Pretend you are a professional singer and sing it.
8. Act extremely bashful while singing, then confident, then sing the song using the same vowel sound for each word.
9. See how much better you feel when you are done!

Sing, sing a song
Sing out loud
Sing out strong
Sing of good things not bad
Sing of happy not sad

Sing, sing a song
Make it simple to last
Your whole life long
Don't worry that it's
Not good enough for anyone else to hear
Just sing, sing a song.

Songwriters: Joseph G. Raposo
Sing Lyrics ©Sony/ATV Music Publishing LLC